For Tabitha, who was
happy to find cheese AS

For the Brealeys,
much love NE

EGMONT
We bring stories to life

First published in Great Britain 2015 by Egmont UK Limited
This edition published 2018 by Dean, an imprint of Egmont UK
Limited, The Yellow Building, 1 Nicholas Road, London, W11 4AN
www.egmont.co.uk

Text copyright © Amy Sparkes 2015
Illustrations copyright © Nick East 2015

Amy Sparkes and Nick East have asserted their moral rights.

ISBN 978 0 6035 7574 7

70174/001

Printed in Malaysia

A CIP catalogue record for this title is available from the
British Library.

Egmont takes its responsibility to the planet and its
inhabitants very seriously. All the papers we use are from
well-managed forests run by responsible suppliers.

SAY·CHEESE · QUALITY CHEESES

NO CHEESE

OUT OF CHEESE

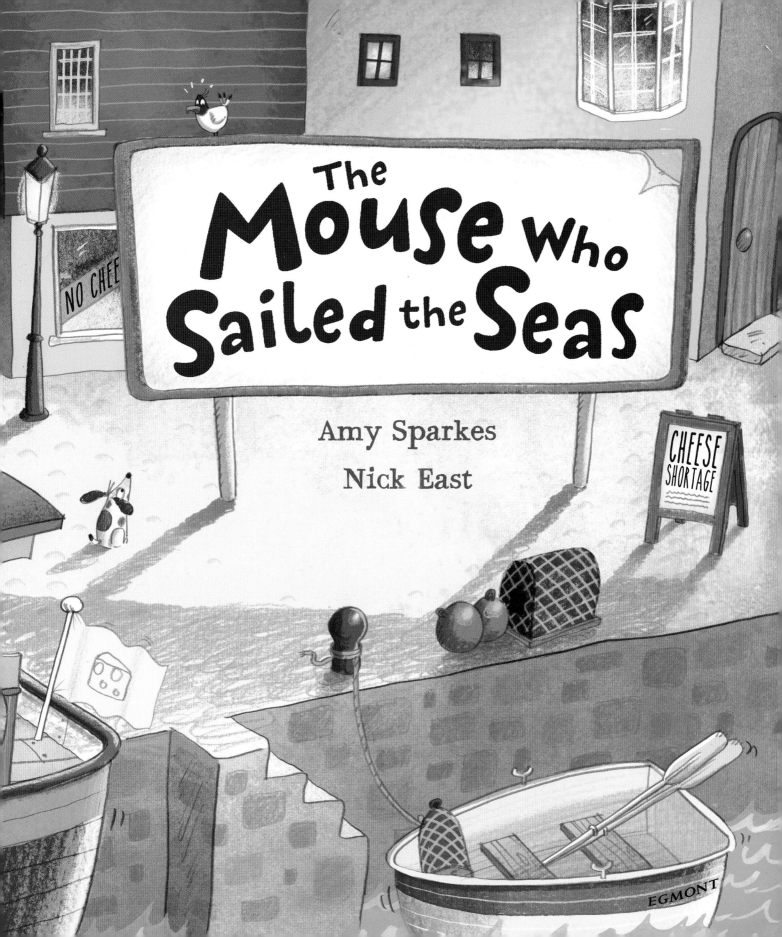

The Mouse Who Sailed the Seas

Amy Sparkes

Nick East

NO CHEE[SE]

CHEESE SHORTAGE

EGMONT

THREE
LOST
BEES

A mouse he went to sail the seas.
He sailed the seas
    to look for cheese,
But all he found were . . .

Bumblebees!

Phut! Phut!

A mouse he went
to sail the seas.
He sailed the seas to
look for **cheese**,
But all he found
were bumblebees
And . . .

Aliens like purple peas!

A mouse he went to sail the seas.
He sailed the seas to look for **cheese**,

But all he found were bumblebees
And aliens like purple peas
And . . .

Goats with very hairy knees!

A mouse he went to sail the seas.
He sailed the seas to look for **cheese**,

But all he found were bumblebees
And aliens like purple peas
And goats with very hairy knees

And . . .

Elves who had a magic sneeze!

AAAACHOOOOO!

Now, a boat that's
on a quest for cheese,
Piled up high with **bumblebees**

And **aliens**
like purple peas

And **goats** with
very hairy knees

And **elves** who had a
magic sneeze . . .

AAAAAAACHOOOOOO!

Cannot sail the
seas with ease.

There came a noisy,
groaning **CREAK!**
The mouse let out
a worried **SQUEAK!**
For now the boat
began to **LEAK!**

The elves let out
a magic sneeze . . .

The goats with very hairy knees
Nibbled through their ropes with ease.
While the aliens like purple peas . . .

Saved the mouse
who searched for cheese.

Then pulled up by the bumblebees,
Mouse floated high above the seas . . .

Beyond the sky, above the breeze,
He sailed up into space with ease.

MOON

Until he found . . .

A land of cheese!